Everybody Needs a Hideaway

Written and Illustrated by
Dean Bennett

Down East Books
Camden, Maine

Author's Note

When Boo Dog was a puppy, I built the tree house in this story.
Throughout his long life, we took many trips to our hideaway,
along a trail that I had made through the woods and beside a
brook. Many of the events in the story are true, but one, especially, inspired me to create this book. On one sunny afternoon, I
was in my hideaway, and Boo Dog was asleep on the ground
at the foot of the tree-house ladder. A big moose came out of the
woods on the other side of the bog. It walked toward my tree
house, but before it got to us, it bedded down in a grassy place
near a dead tree.

Boo Dog slept soundly through it all. A short time later, I
sneaked down the ladder, took him by his collar, and together we
walked quietly back along the trail to our house. The moose and
Boo Dog never knew that each other was close by.

Today, I continue to go to my tree-house hideaway, and
although Boo Dog is now gone, he is still with me in spirit. It is
easy to imagine that he is at the foot of the tree, waiting for me
to climb down.

Dean Bennett,
Mount Vernon, Maine

Design by Lindy Gifford

Printed in China

5 4 3 2 1

ISBN 0-89272-645-8

Library of Congress Control Number 2004110913

Down East Books
P.O. Box 679
Camden, ME 04843

A division of Down East Enterprise, publishers of *Down East* magazine, www.downeast.com

To request a book catalog or place an order, visit www.downeastbooks.com, or call 800-685-7962.

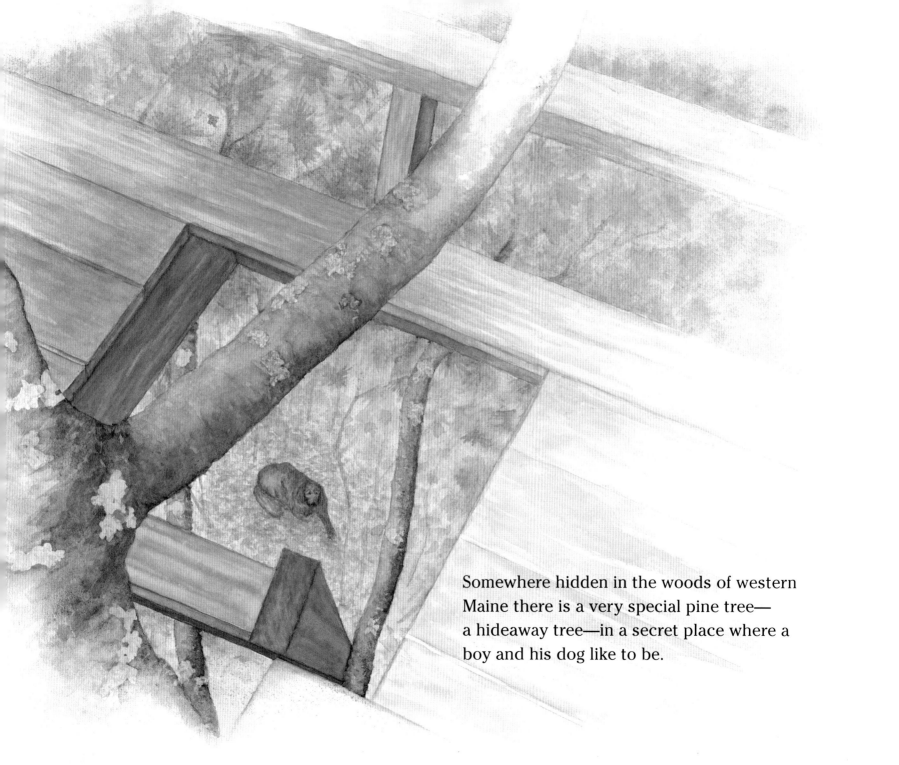

Somewhere hidden in the woods of western
Maine there is a very special pine tree—
a hideaway tree—in a secret place where a
boy and his dog like to be.

After school one fall day, the boy goes alone to
his hideaway and begins to climb a tall wooden
ladder to the top of the big tree, where Chickadee
welcomes him, whirring from branch to branch.

The boy moves up through an opening in the hideaway's floor, then he looks out to see Flicker in the top of a nearby dead tree. Here, the big woodpecker once used its powerful beak to make a deep hole where it safely raised a family of downy nestlings.

High up in his secret hiding spot, the boy sits quietly, watching Beaver's world below—a boggy place of water and grass and dead trees. Beaver cut down some of the nearby birch trees using his huge front teeth so that he could get at the tender bark of their upper branches. Then, just as it is getting late in the day, the boy's heartbeat quickens. He sees Bull Moose coming toward his tree.

To the boy's surprise, the great dark animal stops right beneath his hideaway. The moose looks slowly around, swinging its broad antlers. Suddenly, with a big sigh, it lowers itself onto the bed of soft pine needles that cover the ground. The boy begins to worry, for he is afraid to climb down, and he is expected at home.

Not far away from the boy, now trapped in his hideaway tree, the late-afternoon sun shines through the window of a house, onto a table that is already set for supper. Stretched out on the floor of the kitchen, a golden red dog feels the light touch of a woman's hand. "Boo Dog, go fetch Ben," the boy's mother softly commands.

The dog bounds away across a field, its grass now yellow in the dryness of the fall season. Perched high in a tall maple tree overlooking the grassy patch of land, Crow sees the dog running. All summer, the big black bird had hunted the field for insects and had often seen the dog and the boy come and go, following the trail below, the path that led to the hideaway tree.

At the edge of a forest, Ruffed Grouse hears Boo Dog's approach, and with a startling roar of wings, the bird flies up from a dusting hollow beneath its apple-tree roost. The curious dog stops to sniff and finds a feather that tickles his nose. But he can't stay for long because he has a job to do.

A few steps away, Boo Dog catches a whiff of
a wild smell that's very fresh, and he sees two
pointed puddles, shining like mirrors on a patch
of ground that's squishy and wet. These are Bull
Moose's tracks, and they are headed in the same
direction as the dog.

Moose's tracks lead through a thicket into dark woods, where Red Squirrel is dining on the fallen cones of white pines. Boo Dog makes a wild dash for the small animal, but it leaps to safety in a tall tree. The dog stops to look and listen, but the squirrel is hiding, and all is quiet except for the whisper of a breeze.

Beyond the pines, a bubbling brook gurgles noisily
as it bounces down over its rocky bed, washing
away Bull Moose's huge hoofprints. Boo Dog
stops to drink and sees a leaf float by with a
strange little ball attached to its top. This is a gall,
the empty home of Wasp, who once lived safely
inside, high among the leaves of a tall oak tree.

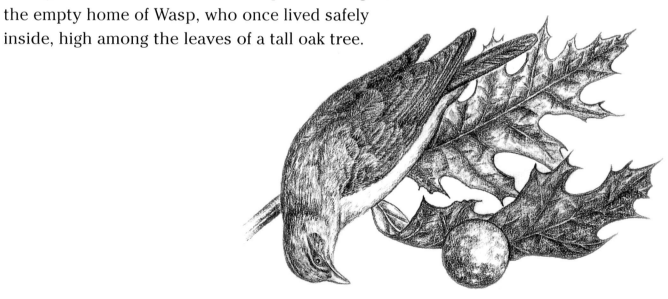

Woolly Bear caterpillar slowly ripples across Boo Dog's path, and the playful dog nudges it along with his nose. The caterpillar is looking for a home in an old hollow log, where it will be safe from the coming snows. Next spring, on some warm day, a tiger moth will crawl out of Woolly Bear's protective cocoon and flutter away.

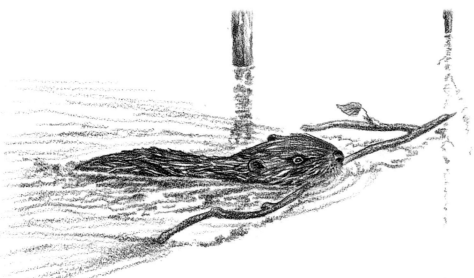

Boo Dog approaches the edge of the brook where it flows quietly, its calm waters reflecting the darkening sky. Here, a long time ago, beavers cut down a big tree and used its branches to build a house of mud and sticks in the middle of the bog. Now the old tree trunk makes a bridge where Boo Dog and the boy can keep dry when they cross the brook.

At last Boo Dog comes to the ladder leaning against the tall pine. He looks up into the tree but can only see the boy's shoes. Then his nose catches a strong moosey smell, and he sees something odd. It looks like a gigantic nose sticking out from behind the hideaway tree. Then the nose moves!

Boo Dog gives his fiercest, loudest bark, although it ends on a note of fright. The big moose comes awkwardly to his feet, for Boo Dog is not the only one who is startled and alarmed. With only so much as a glance at the quivering dog, the big animal turns and, in a flurry of flying leaves and pounding hooves, crashes off through the woods, out of sight.

Down the ladder the boy scrambles, giving Boo Dog the biggest hug he ever got, for the boy now knows what a special friend his dog has been. He also knows that there can be times when *everybody* needs a hideaway, and for some, like Red Squirrel or Wasp or Chickadee—or even a person like you or me—it could be a tree.

Acknowledgments

I wrote and illustrated the first draft of this book in 1987, and through the ensuing years, I continued to work on the presentation of the story and the artwork, seeking direction from children, parents, teachers, and other authors and artists. I thank the many people who helped me along the way, especially the following: Dawna Lisa Buchanan-Berrigan, Carolyn Corbin, Carole Godomsky, Stephen Godomsky, J. Thomas R. Higgins, Sharon LeBlond, Valerie MacDowell, Mark Melnicove, Marcia Nash, Jeanne Smedberg, and the many children who told me how they felt about the book. I also thank my editor, Chris Cornell, for his keen eye and strong support. Finally, I thank my wife, Sheila, and my son, Richard, for their advice and encouragement. And, of course, I thank Boo Dog, a friend beyond words and the golden retriever who made this story possible.